Shadow

JILL NEWSOME

ILLUSTRATED BY CLAUDIO MUÑOZ

www.dk.com

LONDON • NEW YORK • SYDNEY • STUTTGART

To Isabel

www.dk.com

First published in Great Britain in 1999
by Dorling Kindersley Limited,
9 Henrietta Street, London WC2E 8PS

2 4 6 8 10 9 7 5 3 2 1

A CIP catalogue record for this book is available from the British Library.
ISBN 0-7513-7435-0
Colour reproduction by Dot Gradations, UK
Printed and bound in China by L. Rex Ltd.

My name is Rosy.
Everything was fine –
my home, my school, my friends.
Until the day we moved.

That day,
my whole
world turned
upside down.

Nothing I did seemed
right anymore. People
started to say how rude
and bad-tempered I was.

Every day Dad walked me to my new school through the wood behind our new house. It was dark and spooky, and I didn't like it one bit.

Everyone at my new school looked so strange, I wished I was really tiny so I could hide in my dad's arms.

There were nights when I just couldn't go to sleep. My dreams were scary. How I missed all my friends and my old home!

One day snow was falling
so school closed early.

We walked home slowly,
watching the silent wood
in the swirling snow.

All of a sudden, I saw a little face – a rabbit lying quite still, looking at me.

I saw that it was hurt, so very carefully
I picked it up and carried it home.

Everyone agreed the rabbit could stay.

Mum helped me take care of
the rabbit's hurt leg.

Dad helped me make a cosy
hutch for its new home.

Before long, the rabbit was feeling well
enough to hop around the house. It followed
me everywhere, so I called it Shadow.

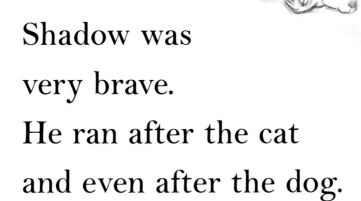

Shadow was
very brave.
He ran after the cat
and even after the dog.

We played
hide-and-seek
together. We
had lots of fun.

But one day Shadow disappeared.
I looked in every room in our house
and all over the neighbourhood.

At suppertime, I wasn't hungry.
All I could think about was how
much I missed Shadow.

What would I do without my new friend?

Suddenly, I had an idea.

I got some paper
and began
to write:

Just then, the doorbell rang.
It was Nancy, a girl from my
class, holding a huge box.

Inside, there was Shadow!

Now Nancy and I walk to school together.
We play at each other's houses and in the
wood, which is not spooky anymore.

And sometimes
Shadow comes too.